D0411329

Supper is late, and Snoopy gets worried.
Are his friends in trouble? He sets off to look
for them, and Woodstock goes too.

Acknowledgment:
Background artwork and design by Gaynor Berry

British Library Cataloguing in Publication Data

Volke, Gordon
    Snoopy to the rescue.
    I. Title   II. Schulz, Charles M. (Charles Monroe) *1922 –*
    813.54 [J]
    ISBN 0-7214-1438-9

First edition

Published by Ladybird Books Ltd Loughborough Leicestershire UK
Ladybird Books Inc Auburn Maine 04210 USA

Printed in England (3)

snoopy
to the rescue

by Gordon Volke

Based on the characters
created by Charles M Schulz

Ladybird Books

Snoopy was asleep on top of his doghouse. He had been there all afternoon. "My tummy clock tells me it's nearly suppertime,"
                    thought Snoopy, dreamily.

KLUNK!

Suddenly something tickled Snoopy's nose.

"ATISHOO!" Snoopy gave an enormous sneeze and fell head-first off his doghouse!

"What made me do that?" wondered Snoopy, holding his head.

Just then a small yellow feather
floated past Snoopy's face. It was
followed by another, and another.
"So that's it!" cried Snoopy.

Woodstock was moulting!

"Just stay behind me, Woodstock.
I don't want feathers in my face,"
said Snoopy.

Snoopy's tummy gave a loud rumble. "Suppertime!" he exclaimed.

The hungry beagle jumped back on his doghouse and waited for the back door to open, but Charlie Brown did not appear with his supper dish. "That's strange," thought Snoopy.

After a while, he knocked on the back door. To his surprise it creaked open. Snoopy went inside and looked around, but there was no sign of Charlie Brown or Sally.

"I wonder what's going on?" murmured Snoopy.

Then he spotted
a note. It said:

> *Dear Snoopy,*
> *Sally and I have gone*
> *to the park to play with*
> *Peppermint Patty and*
> *Schroeder. Afterwards*
> *we're going to the maze.*
> *See you at suppertime.*
> *Love,*
> *Charlie Brown*

"They're late!"
thought Snoopy, anxiously.

Snoopy waited and waited, but still his friends did not appear.

"I'd better go and look for them," he thought.

Outside in the garden, Snoopy spotted Charlie Brown's skateboard.

"Just what I need!" he chuckled.
Snoopy sped off on the skateboard
with Woodstock fluttering
along behind.
If there was
anything
in the way,
Snoopy
jumped over it!

"Call me
Skateboard
Joe!" he
grinned.

Meanwhile, in the park, Snoopy's friends were lost in the maze.

"We've walked this way and that way and we *still* can't find our way out," sighed Charlie Brown. "What are we going to do?"

Schroeder had an idea. "If I play my piano," he cried, "people will hear the music and rescue us!"

"Good idea!" agreed the others.

So Schroeder sat down at the keys and began to play.

Unfortunately,
Schroeder chose
a lullaby. "What
lovely music,"
muttered Peppermint
Patty, closing her
eyes. Soon her
head began to
nod and she started to snore.

"My idea's not working,"
sighed Schroeder.
"I'm sending
everyone to sleep."

Patty woke up with a start.
"I know what to do instead!"
she said, picking up her baseball bat.

Patty told Charlie Brown to tie a
note to their baseball. "Now toss it
to me and I'll whack it right out of
the maze," she cried. "Someone
will soon find it!"

THWACK! Patty hit the ball first time and it sailed into the sky. "That should reach one of our gardens!" she smiled.

In fact, the baseball came down in Charlie Brown's garden – right in Woodstock's birdbath!

The message sank without trace!

The children waited patiently, but of course nothing happened.

"I've got another plan," said
Charlie Brown. "We'll write 'HELP'
on my kite and fly it above
the maze."

It was a good plan, but Charlie
Brown was hopeless at kite flying!
He ran up and down jerking at the
kite string. "Can't get it off the
ground!" he puffed.

A sudden gust of wind caught the
kite and lifted it into the air.
"WHOA!" yelled Charlie Brown,
hanging onto the string. SNAP!
The string broke and the kite blew
away, getting stuck in the branches
of a tree.

"Good grief! The kite-eating tree
has struck again!"
groaned Charlie Brown.

Now there seemed no way of escape. "S-S-Suppose we have to stay here all night," stammered Sally. "There m-m-might be a monster in the maze!"

Next moment, shuffling footsteps were heard approaching. "Here it comes now!" wailed Sally.

A familiar figure came trotting round the corner.

"Snoopy!" everyone cried.

The clever beagle had made his way to the centre of the maze, carefully remembering every twist and turn.

"Come on," cried Peppermint Patty. "Snoopy knows the way out!"

Soon everyone was out of the maze.

"HURRAY!" cheered Charlie Brown. "We're free at last!" The children were tired and hungry, so they set off for home. Snoopy started to follow them.

An urgent cheeping
made him stop.
"That's Woodstock!"
gasped Snoopy.

The little bird was still
inside the maze.
"I told Woodstock
to stay behind me!"
exclaimed Snoopy. "He must
have been following me all
the time!"

Snoopy rushed back into the maze
and found Woodstock.

"Follow me," he said
to his little friend.
"I'll lead you out, too."

Snoopy led Woodstock towards what he thought was the exit, but there was no way out. "Must be this way," he called, changing direction. There was no way out there, either!

"I didn't look where I was going!" groaned Snoopy. "Now *we're* lost!"

Snoopy and Woodstock wandered round in circles, growing more and more confused. In the end they gave up and sat down. "We'll have to spend the night here," sighed Snoopy. "And I still haven't had my supper!"

Then Snoopy spotted some yellow feathers lying on the ground. As Woodstock had walked through the maze, he had left a trail of feathers behind him.

Snoopy jumped to his feet.

"Come on, Woodstock!" he cried. "Follow those feathers!"

The trail of feathers led Snoopy and Woodstock back through the maze. They got out the way they had come in.

When the two friends were safely back in the park, they gave a little dance of joy!

At home, Snoopy and Woodstock
found Charlie Brown waiting with
Snoopy's supper and a special plate
of chocolate chip cookies.

Snoopy picked up Woodstock and
gave him a hug. "I rescued Charlie
Brown and his friends," he thought,
"but I needed Woodstock to rescue
me!"

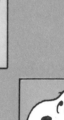